Dear Parents:

Congratulations! Your child is taking the first steps on an exciting journey. The destination? Independent reading!

STEP INTO READING® will help your child get there. The program offers five steps to reading success. Each step includes fun stories and colorful art or photographs. In addition to original fiction and books with favorite characters, there are Step into Reading Non-Fiction Readers, Phonics Readers and Boxed Sets, Sticker Readers, and Comic Readers—a complete literacy program with something to interest every child.

Learning to Read, Step by Step!

Ready to Read   Preschool–Kindergarten
• big type and easy words • rhyme and rhythm • picture clues
For children who know the alphabet and are eager to begin reading.

Reading with Help   Preschool–Grade 1
• basic vocabulary • short sentences • simple stories
For children who recognize familiar words and sound out new words with help.

Reading on Your Own   Grades 1–3
• engaging characters • easy-to-follow plots • popular topics
For children who are ready to read on their own.

Reading Paragraphs   Grades 2–3
• challenging vocabulary • short paragraphs • exciting stories
For newly independent readers who read simple sentences with confidence.

Ready for Chapters   Grades 2–4
• chapters • longer paragraphs • full-color art
For children who want to take the plunge into chapter books but still like colorful pictures.

STEP INTO READING® is designed to give every child a successful reading experience. The grade levels are only guides; children will progress through the steps at their own speed, developing confidence in their reading.

Remember, a lifetime love of reading starts with a single step!

Visit us on the Web!
StepIntoReading.com
randomhousekids.com

Educators and librarians, for a variety of teaching tools, visit us at
RHTeachersLibrarians.com

ISBN 978-0-7364-3093-7 (trade) — ISBN 978-0-7364-8146-5 (lib. bdg.) —
ISBN 978-0-7364-3204-7 (ebook)

Printed in the United States of America
10 9 8 7 6 5 4 3 2 1

Disney · PIXAR

THE GOOD DINOSAUR

The Journey Home

By Bill Scollon

Illustrated by the Disney Storybook Art Team

Random House 🏠 New York

Arlo is a dinosaur.
He lives
with his family
on a farm.

Arlo is scared
of many things.
He is afraid
to leave the farm.

A wild boy steals food!

Arlo is scared.

He runs away.

Arlo and the boy
fall into the river.
The water sweeps
them away.

Arlo is far
from home.
The boy is gone.

Arlo is lost.

He is scared.

Arlo can follow the river
to get home.

The boy finds Arlo.

He brings food.

Arlo follows the boy
into the woods.

Arlo names the boy Spot.

They have fun together.

They become friends.

Arlo and Spot get lost.

They are attacked!

A pack of T. rexes
saves them.

Arlo and Spot are happy.

They will be home soon.

A human calls

to Spot.

Arlo is afraid that

Spot might leave.

But he stays with Arlo.

Arlo and Spot

are attacked again!

Spot is trapped

in a log.

This time,
Arlo is brave.
He fights
to help Spot.

A flash flood
is coming!
It almost carries
Spot away.

Arlo jumps
into the water.
He will save
his friend!

Arlo and Spot go
over a waterfall.
They swim to shore.
They are safe!

Spot meets a human family.

Arlo knows Spot should stay
with them.

Arlo and Spot say goodbye.

Arlo is a brave dinosaur.
He finds the farm
on his own.
Arlo is home!